By Emily Thompson

Illustrated by Tom Leigh

Dalmatian Press, LLC, 2012. All rights reserved.
Published by Dalmatian Press, LLC, 2012. The DALMATIAN PRESS name and logo are trademarks of Dalmatian Press, LLC, Franklin, Tennessee 37067. 1-866-418-2572. No part of this book may be reproduced or copied in any form without written permission from the copyright owner.

Printed in the U.S.A.
ISBN: 1-40375-322-9

12 13 14 15 BM 37693 10 9 8 7 6 5
17930

1 One tire...

...makes a swing.

2 Two pieces of bread...

...make a sandwich.

3 Three snowballs...

...make a snowman.

4 Four letters…

...make Elmo's name.

5 Five musicians...

...make a jazzy band.

6 Six friends make a pyramid.

7 Seven stars make the Big Dipper.

8 Eight patches...

...make Elmo's quilt.

9 Nine baseball players make a team.

10 Ten monsters…

...make a mess!